FRANKiE SPARKS
AND THE BIG SLED CHALLENGE

ALSO BY
MEGAN FRAZER BLAKEMORE

GRADE INVENTOR

FRANKIE SPARKS
AND THE BIG SLED CHALLENGE

BOOK 3

BY MEGAN FRAZER BLAKEMORE
ILLUSTRATED BY NADJA SARELL

ALADDIN   NEW YORK LONDON TORONTO SYDNEY NEW DELHI

ALADDIN

An imprint of Simon & Schuster Children's Publishing Division
1230 Avenue of the Americas, New York, New York 10020
First Aladdin hardcover edition November 2019
Text copyright © 2019 by Megan Frazer Blakemore
Illustrations copyright © 2019 by Nadja Sarell
Also available in an Aladdin paperback edition.
For information about special discounts for bulk purchases, please contact
Simon & Schuster Special Sales at 1-866-506-1949 or business@simonandschuster.com.
The Simon & Schuster Speakers Bureau can bring authors to your live event.
For more information or to book an event contact the Simon & Schuster Speakers Bureau
at 1-866-248-3049 or visit our website at www.simonspeakers.com.
Series designed by Laura Lyn DiSiena
Interior designed by Tiara Iandiorio
The illustrations for this book were rendered in pencil line on paper and digital flat tones.
The text of this book was set in Nunito.
Manufactured in the United States of America 0920 QVE
10 9 8 7 6 5 4 3 2
Library of Congress Cataloging-in-Publication Data
Names: Blakemore, Megan Frazer, author. | Sarell, Nadja, illustrator.
Title: Frankie Sparks and the big sled challenge /
by Megan Frazer Blakemore; illustrated by Nadja Sarell.
Description: First Aladdin paperback edition. | New York : Aladdin, 2019. | Series: Frankie
Sparks, third-grade inventor ; 3 | Summary: Frankie Sparks is excited about her town's team
sled design contest but while she knows a lot about building a sled, she has much to learn
about building a team. Includes information on the design process and a challenge.
Identifiers: LCCN 2019007936 (print) | LCCN 2019010446 (eBook) |
ISBN 9781534430518 (eBook) | ISBN 9781534430501 (hc) | ISBN 9781534430495 (pbk)
Subjects: | CYAC: Contests—Fiction. | Cooperativeness—Fiction. | Sleds—Fiction. |
Friendship—Fiction. | Inventions—Fiction. | BISAC: JUVENILE FICTION /
Sports & Recreation / Winter Sports. | JUVENILE FICTION / Social Issues / New Experience.
| JUVENILE FICTION / Science & Technology.
Classification: LCC PZ7.B574 (eBook) | LCC PZ7.B574 Fk 2019 (print) |
DDC [Fic]—dc23
LC record available at https://lccn.loc.gov/2019007936

Dedicated to Margaret Burman,
who knows a thing or two about
building with cardboard,
and about a million more things
about being a good teacher,
colleague, and friend

CONTENTS

CONTENTS

FRANKIE SPARKS AND THE BIG SLED CHALLENGE

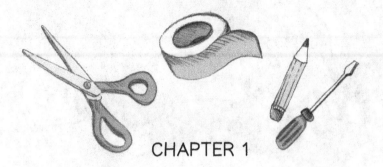

CHAPTER 1

Extreme Maximus Jump

WHOOSH!

The wind whipped past Frankie's face. She held on tightly to the handles on her red saucer sled as she flew down the snowy hill.

Bump, bump, bump! She went over a patch of chunky snow that rattled her teeth and shook her brain inside her head.

Her big challenge was coming up quickly.

Everyone called it Extreme Maximus. Once, a fifth grader had gone off it, flown three feet in the air, and done a flip! At least, that's what people said.

Most of the third graders were too scared to try Extreme Maximus. They stayed in the center of the hill. But not Frankie. She was built for speed. She thrived on action. She was going to conquer Extreme Maximus.

This was her third time trying. The first two times, she'd gotten scared and bailed out at the last minute. Not this time. She squeezed the handles even more tightly.

"Go, Frankie!" her best friend, Maya, yelled from the bottom of the hill. Now Frankie definitely couldn't chicken out. Not with people watching.

She was practically on top of the jump. She closed her eyes as tightly as she could.

Up, up, up she flew, and then . . .

Crash!

Her saucer landed hard and started spinning around and around. She opened her eyes to a whirl of white snow, green trees, and blue sky.

She coasted along a bit longer and then thumped up against the bench that was near the bottom of the hill.

"Oof!" she exclaimed. She was pretty sure she'd left her stomach somewhere behind her. She rolled off the sled and onto the snow. She still felt like she was spinning.

Maya ran up to her. "Frankie, are you okay?"

Frankie popped up. "Okay? I am awesome! I conquered Extreme Maximus!"

Luke, who was in their class, came running over. "That was *epic*, Frankie!"

"I know!" she replied.

"You're the first third grader *ever* to go over Extreme Maximus!" Luke was clearly impressed, which made Frankie's chest puff up.

"You should have seen yourself," Maya said. "I think you got a full foot off the ground!"

A foot? Frankie was pretty sure she had gone much higher than that. Three feet, at least, but probably four. It was hard to say since she had kept her eyes closed, but it had *felt* like she was really high.

"Totally cool," Luke said. He looked up the hill a little wistfully.

Frankie picked up her sled. "Yeah, it was pretty cool. When you're a real thrill seeker like me, though, it's all in a day's work."

"Is that why you jumped off your sled the first two times?"

Frankie startled. It was Lila Jones, her classmate and one of her not-so-favorite people. Where had Lila even come from?

"I just wanted to make sure I had the angle right for the best trajectory," Frankie told her.

Lila looked confused at the word "trajectory." It was one of Frankie's favorite words. She'd learned it when she'd built a rocket. The trajectory was the path an object took when it went up and down. Her rocket's trajectory had been straight up thirty feet, then a perfect arc, then a crash landing in the field outside Grace

Hopper Elementary. Thankfully, Frankie's own trajectory had ended in a much softer landing.

"It was definitely amazing, Frankie," Maya said. "I don't think I'll ever go off that jump."

"You could do it, Maya," Frankie told her. Frankie wasn't actually sure that Maya could go off the jump, but Frankie thought it was a nice thing to say. She pushed one of her curls, damp with melting snow, out of her face. "I think once was enough for me for today, though. Want to go back over to the less steep side of the hill?"

"Sure," Maya said, looking a little relieved. "Are you guys coming?" Maya asked Lila and Luke.

"I would," Lila said. "But I need to put my team together for the contest."

Frankie's ears pricked up. Contest? There were few things she liked more than a contest. Once, she'd won a whole jar of jelly beans by guessing, correctly, that there were 1,197 in the jar. "What contest?" she asked.

"The sled contest," Lila said, as if that answered the question. Lila took a peppermint out of her pocket and carefully unwrapped it. Frankie was pretty sure Lila was doing this

on purpose, just to drag out the moment and make Frankie wait.

Frankie hopped from foot to foot.

With the mint in her mouth and garbling her words a little bit, Lila said, "There's a poster about it over by the hot-chocolate stand. The recreation department is having a contest to see who can build the best sled and—"

Frankie didn't wait to hear the rest of what Lila had to say. She was off and running. A sled-*building* contest? Frankie couldn't believe how perfect it was. Frankie Sparks was the world's greatest third-grade inventor, and she was definitely going to win this contest.

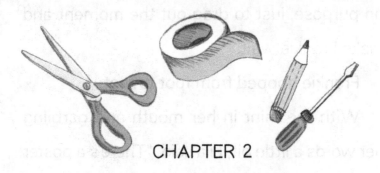

CHAPTER 2

The Contest

FRANKIE READ THE POSTER CARE-
fully two times. Reading could be a challenge for Frankie. Sometimes she read too
quickly and missed words. Sometimes she
read words that weren't there or read the
wrong word. Sometimes she got mixed up.
She needed to be sure she got every detail
about this contest just right.

CALLING ALL KIDS!

THIS WINTER VACATION

FARMINGTON RECREATION IS HOSTING

THE FIRST ANNUAL CARDBOARD-SLED CONTEST!

YOUR MISSION:

DESIGN AND BUILD A SLED USING ONLY

CARDBOARD AND DUCT TAPE.

SLEDS WILL BE JUDGED AND PRIZES

WILL BE GIVEN FOR:

1. BEST-LOOKING SLED.

2. FASTEST SLED.

3. MOST TEAM SPIRIT.

MANDATORY INFORMATION AND BUILDING SESSION:

SUNDAY AT 2:00 P.M.

COME WITH YOUR THREE-MEMBER TEAM AND

YOUR AWESOME IDEAS!

A contest with prizes! Frankie hopped up and down with excitement.

Maya ran up behind her, huffing and puffing. "You sure are fast when you wanna be."

Frankie pointed at the poster. "You'll be on my team, right?"

"Of course," Maya replied.

Frankie pulled off her mitten and reached out her hand. Maya looked at it. "We have to shake," Frankie said. "That's how teams start. With a handshake and a dream."

"Okay," Maya said slowly. She reached out her hand, still in its mitten, and Frankie gave it a firm shake.

"We need one more person," Frankie said.

"What about Lila?" Maya asked. "We already know she wants to do it."

Frankie stared at Maya in disbelief. Lila Jones on her team? No way!

"What about Luke?" Frankie asked.

Maya shook her head. "He said he's making a team with Ben and Ben's little brother. They figure he's small, so that will make fitting three people on the sled easier."

Frankie hadn't thought of that. She and Maya were both pretty regular-size. Maybe they should find a smaller teammate. Then again, maybe small wasn't the best option. Heavier things tended to slide faster, Frankie thought, like the big middle schoolers who flew down the hill. Frankie thought of the people in their class at school. She needed someone who was smart, brave, and just the right size.

While she was thinking, their classmate Ravi

came over to them. He had a steaming cup of
hot chocolate that he was blowing on to try to
cool it down. He said hello to them. Maya said

hello back, but Frankie was still thinking. Suki Moskowitz would be perfect. She was very smart, and brave enough. Plus, she was about the same size as Frankie and Maya, so they could distribute their weight evenly. That would be important. Frankie scowled, though, because she bet that Lila had asked Suki already. Still, it was worth a shot. Frankie decided she would go right home and call Suki and ask her.

"That looks like an interesting contest," Ravi said.

"Want to be on our team?" Maya asked.

Ravi? Ravi was definitely smart, but bravery did not jump to mind when Frankie thought of him. He never jumped off the top of the climbing structure at school or went down the slide backward and headfirst. Plus, he was tall. How would they fit him on the sled?

"Sure," Ravi said.

"Great!" Maya said. "We have our team!"

Frankie forced a smile. "Yeah," she said. "That's great. Welcome to the team."

Maya stuck her hand out. "We have to shake on it," she said.

Frankie grimaced but stuck out her own hand. "Handshake and a dream," she muttered.

Ravi, his hand warm from holding the hot chocolate, shook their hands. They stared at one another a moment longer. Then Ravi said, "Okay, then. I guess I'll see you tomorrow at the information and building session."

He wandered away. Maya clapped her hands together. "That worked out perfectly!"

Frankie, though, wasn't so sure.

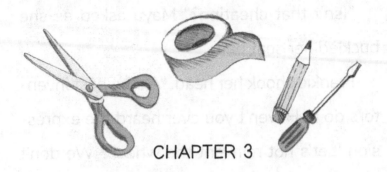

CHAPTER 3

Getting Inspired

WHEN YOU'RE WORKING ON A DESIGN,
it's good to get inspiration from people who
came before you. Frankie explained this to
Maya in the car as they were leaving the sledding hill. Maya was coming over for a sleepover,
which Frankie thought would be a great time
to get going on their sled design. "We can stop
at Magpie's on the way home," Frankie said,
"and look at all the sleds there."

"Isn't that cheating?" Maya asked as she buckled her seat belt.

Frankie shook her head. "All the best inventors do it. Haven't you ever heard the expression 'Let's not reinvent the wheel'? We don't want to reinvent the sled; we just want to make it better."

From the driver's seat, Frankie's mom said, "You will stand on the shoulders of sled-making giants."

Maya gave Frankie a funny look.

"It's Isaac Newton," Frankie explained. "He said that he got so far in the field of physics because he was able to build on what people before him had done."

Frankie's mom drove through town and pulled up in front of Magpie's. The store carried a little bit of everything. The sleds were displayed right out front. Frankie and Maya climbed out of the minivan and rushed toward them.

"Stay by the sleds," Frankie's mom said. "I'm going to go in and see if they have that mac and cheese you like. Plus we need rubber bands and a new bath mat."

"And duct tape!" Frankie exclaimed. "Lots and lots of duct tape."

The selection of sleds was impressive. There were saucer sleds like the one Frankie had, blow-up tube sleds, and old-fashioned sleds with runners. There were long plastic sleds with ridges to help them go more smoothly, and sleds that were no bigger than a kid's bum. There was even a wooden toboggan that was at least six feet long.

"This is going to be a tough choice," Frankie said. "There are pluses and minuses to each design."

She pulled her notebook out of her inside coat pocket. Frankie did not travel anywhere without her little red notebook. She kept a pencil tucked in the spiral at the top.

"Don't you think we should get Ravi's opinion?" Maya asked.

"But Ravi's not here right now, and we are."

"But he's on our team," Maya pointed out.

Frankie was still feeling a little sore about that. She wished she had been able to call Suki first. Suki was really good at art, so they could have won both fastest sled and best-looking sled. What did Ravi bring to the team? Frankie couldn't think of anything. Instead of saying so, she started writing notes in her book. The most important thing, she thought, was figuring out how to make the bottom. There were runners, flat bottoms, and ridges. Runners would probably be hard to make out of cardboard, she thought, but that might make them extra impressive to the judges.

Maya jumped from foot to foot. She blew out air in little white puffs and watched them float away.

"Are you even looking?" Frankie asked.

Maya said, "I like the wooden ones. I think they're nice-looking."

Frankie agreed that they were very nice-looking.

Frankie sketched a few design ideas, and then Maya said, "I'm freezing!"

They decided to wait inside the store, right by the door, where Frankie's mom would see them.

Magpie's smelled like sawdust and cinnamon. Cheery holiday music played overhead. A big display at the front of the store showcased holiday decorations, including a snowman that wiggled and danced to the music. Frankie and Maya started dancing too, giggling together at how silly they looked. There wasn't anything much better than dancing at Magpie's with your best friend, Frankie thought.

That good thought bubble lasted only a second, because just then Lila Jones came around the corner. She wore rolls of duct tape up her arms like bracelets: all the colors of the rainbow plus silver, gold, and black. Her

dad was behind her, holding a stack of empty boxes.

"Hi, Maya!" Lila exclaimed. "Hi, Frankie."

Maya said hello, but Frankie narrowed her eyes and said, "Getting supplies, I see."

"Yep!" Lila said cheerily. Frankie figured that was Lila's game plan. She'd be all cheery and nice, but behind that sweet surface she'd be hatching some evil plan. "Suki, Lauren, and I are going to make the most awesome sled ever."

I knew it! Frankie thought. Lila had scooped up Suki. Lauren was a great person to have on your team too. Her schoolwork was always neat and perfect. That attention to detail would be a big help. Frankie felt like her whole body was getting hot and itchy. She was the best inventor in all of third grade, and probably all of Grace Hopper Elementary. She'd been so sure that she would win any invention contest ever, but how could she beat a dream team like Suki, Lauren, and Lila?

"Fun!" Maya said.

Frankie scowled.

"Are you guys a team?" Lila asked.

Frankie nodded.

"Who with?" Lila asked.

"Ravi," Maya said.

"Maya and I are getting started tonight, though," Frankie said. "We're having a sleepover. We'll probably have the whole thing practically done by tomorrow." She put her hands on her hips.

"Is that allowed?" Lila asked.

"What do you mean?" Frankie replied.

"It says a team of three," Lila said. "I just figured that means you all work on it together. You can't leave anyone out."

"That's what I said," Maya agreed.

Lila's dad jumped in too: "Sounds about

right to me. Three members on a team, three team members working."

"Plus there's that mandatory meeting tomorrow. I figured we couldn't start building until then," Lila said.

It was like a big pig pile of wet cement had been dumped onto Frankie's enthusiasm. Worst of all, she was pretty sure they were right. "We're just brainstorming," she said. "I'm sure everyone is thinking of ideas before tomorrow, and then we will share ideas with our team."

"I guess. Anyway, see you tomorrow," Lila said, and she and her dad walked out of the store.

"Ugh," Frankie groaned when Lila had left. "Why does she have to be so mean?"

"I didn't think she was being mean—" Maya started to say.

"She's *always* being mean," Frankie said with a sigh. "I bet their team already has an idea. I bet it's a good one. I bet—"

"It's no big deal, Frankie," Maya interrupted. "We have that meeting tomorrow, and we can start planning then. We'll be done in no time, with you on our team!"

Frankie wanted to be as optimistic as Maya, but as far as she could tell, Lila's team had a big head start.

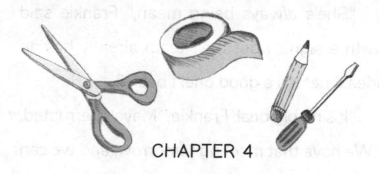

CHAPTER 4

Top-Secret Information

FRANKIE ARRIVED AT THE INFORMA-
tion session seventeen minutes early. No one
else was there. Not Maya. Not Ravi. Not Lila.
Not anyone in charge. She sat down on the
floor of the community room at the rec center.
The walls were covered with posters encour-
aging healthy habits, like FRUITS AND VEGGIES
MAKE YOUR MOUTH SMILE AND YOUR BODY STRONG!

and THE MORE YOU MOVE, THE BETTER YOU FEEL, SO RIDE YOUR BIKE WITH THE SPINNING WHEEL!

Frankie lived by the motto "If you're bored, you're boring." There were a lot of things she could do in seventeen minutes. She could practice her headstands against the wall. Her record was thirty-nine seconds. She could work on her epic plan for a solar-powered popcorn popper. She decided that the best use of her time, though, was to keep thinking about her sled design.

Her mom had told Maya and Frankie that there were three types of sleds you could ride in the Olympics. Sledding in the Olympics! Frankie thought she could be a gold-medal winner in that.

During the sleepover, Frankie had done

some research online while she and Maya had watched a movie with Frankie's parents. The three types of Olympic sleds were bobsled, skeleton, and luge. The coolest were the skeletons, which Frankie thought was a great name. They were used in a race where people ran and dove onto the sled and went down a track face-first. They went up to eighty miles per hour, which was superfast. The bobsleds, though, went even faster. They were almost like go-karts on the ice, and they can speed up to 125 miles per hour. That was faster than most cars!

What the three Olympic sleds had in common were runners along the bottom—blades almost like the ones on ice skates. If that was good enough for the Olympics, Frankie figured it was good enough for her team. In the rec-center community room, she took out her notebook and drew a flat-bottomed sled with two runners. She made the front pointy like a rocket. *Perfect,* she thought. Maybe they could even use colored tape to make it look like a space rocket. That would get them style points!

As she was sketching, people started to come in. Lila, Suki, and Lauren came together and sat right up front. Lila had a notebook and she flipped it open. The three girls whispered together. Only Suki said hello to Frankie.

Maya was close behind. "What's that?" she asked Frankie when she sat down.

"Our sled!"

Maya peered at it more closely. "Cool!" she exclaimed. "It looks like a pencil."

"It's not a pencil; it's a rocket," she said.

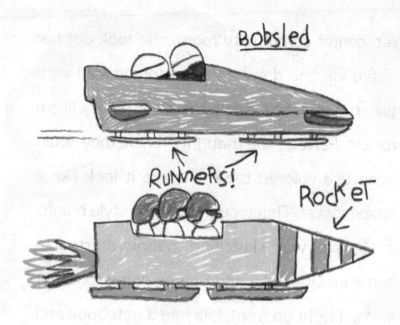

Bobsled

Runners!

Rocket

Ravi came into the room then, wearing a hat with earflaps. He didn't take his hat off when he sat down next to Frankie. "Cool pencil sled," he told her.

"It's not a pencil!" Frankie said. "It's a rocket."

"Does it fly?" he asked.

"Of course not," Frankie replied, though for a moment she let herself imagine launching off Extreme Maximus and shooting right into space. That would be pretty awesome.

Before she could get all the way to the moon in her mind, Ms. Christine from the rec center came into the room. She was wearing her winter hat and a really cool belt with rolls of duct tape attached to it. Frankie wished she had remembered to bring her tool belt.

There were about twenty kids at the meeting. Ms. Christine stood at the front of the room, silent, and, like magic, all the kids quieted down. "Welcome to the pre-race meeting for the first annual cardboard-sled contest!"

Everyone clapped. Frankie clapped hardest of all.

"Okay, so here's the deal," Ms. Christine said. She sat down on a table at the front of the room and swung her feet back and forth. "This contest is all about teamwork and creativity, which are two of my favorite things. It's also all about fun. Got it?"

"Got it!" the kids yelled back.

But, Frankie thought, *it's also about winning.* Maya had her swim team, where she got to show how good she was. Lila and Suki played soccer. Ravi's mom took him all over the state playing in music competitions. Frankie's thing was inventing, and finally there was a contest for her. She was going to be able to prove that she really was the greatest third-grade inventor . . . unless Lila and the other girls got in her way.

"So here's what we're going to do. First, official sign-ups." Ms. Christine held up a clipboard. "Put down all your names and a team

name." She handed the clipboard to Luke, who

sat with his teammates at the side of the room.

"Next, we will go over the rules."

Luke handed the sign-up sheet to Frankie.

She concentrated and carefully wrote down all three of their names: *Frankie, Maya, Ravi*. There was a place for a team name, too, so she wrote down *The Rocket Squad*. She passed the paper to Maya to pass to Lila. Maya hesitated.

"You wrote our team name?" Maya whispered.

Frankie nodded. She was trying to pay attention to Ms. Christine. She didn't want to miss even one detail. Maya frowned and handed the paper to Lila.

"After the rules, we're going to start building," Ms. Christine told them.

Frankie's heart sped up a little bit at that. She lived for building.

"Faroni Appliances has donated boxes for us to use. There are boxes waiting for you in the hallway." She reached down and picked up a huge tote bag. "And this is full of duct tape. Plus I see that many of you brought your own, which is awesome. You can start your sleds here today, and you can come in any time this week to work on them, as long as the rec center is open, of course."

"Can we bring them home?" Frankie asked.

"That's up to your parents. If someone can bring it home for you, you can work on it there, too." She smiled at Frankie. "I think that's a good jumping-off point to talk about the rules."

Ravi had a sketchbook, and he was drawing in it while Ms. Christine was talking. The drawing had nothing to do with sleds as far as Frankie could tell. It looked like he was drawing knights and elves and things like that. Frankie nudged him. This was really important stuff. The rules were their *parameters*: what they could and could not do. Frankie noticed that Lila was writing down everything that Ms. Christine said, so Frankie handed Maya her notebook and pencil. "Can you write?" she whispered.

Maya had beautiful handwriting. Frankie's handwriting was a little messy, and she often spelled words wrong. When Ms. Christine was finished, Maya handed the list back to Frankie, and Frankie read it over. Maya had written everything down in complete sentences.

You have one week to build your sled.

You may use paint or markers for decoration.

Teams must have three members.

Your sled must be no larger than six feet long and two feet wide.

All team members must fit on the sled.

You may not use glue, wax, or any tape other than duct tape in your construction.

You may not use paper, foam, or any material other than cardboard and duct tape.

Next Ms. Christine started explaining the best methods for building with cardboard. She talked about the different ways pieces of cardboard could be attached together: slot and tab, folds, flanges, and more. None of this was news to Frankie. She had about a million tricks for putting cardboard together. She had built many structures out of it: a castle, a boat, a marble maze.

Frankie squirmed. It was like everything she knew about cardboard was itching to get out. Frankie liked knowing things, and she liked sharing what she knew. Frankie shot her hand into the air. But when Ms. Christine called on her, Lila turned around. She had her notebook in her hand and her pencil ready to write. Frankie realized that if she told others how to build with cardboard, she'd be giving up her advantage. "Um, never mind," Frankie said.

Frankie felt a little bad about not sharing her knowledge, but it was a contest, after all. Good ideas were top-secret information. She told her stomach to stop twisting around like a dirty old sponge. She had worked hard to learn so much about building; there was no reason she had to share that knowledge with anyone else. She was the world's greatest third-grade inventor, and this contest was her chance to prove it.

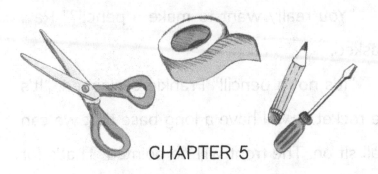

CHAPTER 5

Getting Started

"HERE'S THE PLAN," FRANKIE ANNOUNCED as she spread her drawings out over the floor in the corner of the recreation-center meeting room. Frankie wanted to be able to see everyone else, but not let them see her group. She didn't want anyone to steal her ideas. Maya and Ravi peered down at her drawings. There were about a dozen sketches showing all different angles of the sled Frankie wanted to make.

"You really want to make a pencil?" Ravi asked.

"It's not a pencil!" Frankie exclaimed. "It's a rocket. It will have a long base that we can all sit on. The front will be pointed. That's for aerodynamics. We're going to put runners on the bottom. I looked at pictures of bobsleds and skeletons and those sleds that dogs pull. They all have runners on the bottom. There's less friction that way."

"Less what?" Maya asked.

"Friction. Like when you rub your hands together and they get hot?"

Ravi and Maya both rubbed their palms together.

"That's friction," Frankie said. "And it slows things down."

Ravi straightened up the drawings so they were all in a neat row. He regarded them carefully. "Cool," he said.

"Good! So first we—" Frankie began.

"But," Ravi interrupted, "I kind of wanted our sled to look like a dragon." He pulled a folded-up shiny brochure from his pocket and smoothed it out on the floor. It was from Adventure Fun Park, the local amusement park. Frankie loved Adventure Fun Park! One of her many dream jobs was roller-coaster inventor.

Ravi flipped open the brochure and pointed to the flume ride. Each of the fake logs in the ride had been carved to look like a different dragon. "Like one of these," he said.

"But we aren't the Dragon Squad; we're

the Rocket Squad. That's our team name," Frankie said.

"What?" Ravi asked. "Says who?"

"Says Frankie," Maya said. "She wrote it on the sheet."

"Isn't that something we should've decided together?" Ravi asked. "I was thinking we could be the knights of something."

"The Knights of Something? What kind of name is that?"

"Well, I wasn't sure what the 'something' would be," Ravi said. "I thought we could come up with that together. If we all liked it, I mean."

"I like it," Maya said. "What do you think, Frankie?"

"I think dragons aren't very aerodynamic," Frankie said. She peered over at Luke's group.

Instead of working, they seemed to just be sitting in their refrigerator box and laughing.

"They fly," Ravi said. "By definition they're aerodynamic."

Maya piped up. "Can you tell me what 'aerodynamic' means again?"

Ravi and Frankie both started talking at once. They used their arms to make points and pretend wings. Maya looked from one to the other, trying to follow them both at the same time. Finally she said, "Stop! One at a time, okay?"

Before Frankie could speak, Ravi said, "Basically it means that something goes through the air well." He held up his hand like he was waving to her. "My hand like this wouldn't be aerodynamic because all the wind would hit it."

Frankie held her arm out in front of her, her fingers squeezed together and pointing forward, palm to the floor. "But my hand like this is aerodynamic because the wind can go right around it. Which is why we need to have a pointy front. So we can have the fastest sled."

Maya seemed to understand. "I was actually hoping we could make one that looked like the toboggan we saw."

"Very traditional," Ravi said.

"But if we want to win best-looking sled, we need to do something more creative," Frankie said.

"Like a dragon," Ravi said.

Frankie slapped her head. "No! More creative like *smart*. Like rocket engineers."

"Maybe we should wait on figuring out the front until we have the base?" Maya suggested.

Frankie reluctantly agreed. Everyone knew she was the best inventor, didn't they? They should just listen to her! Maya went to the table to choose tape, while Frankie went for scissors. On the way back, Frankie walked by Lila's group. They also had a refrigerator box, and Ms. Christine was using a box cutter to help them cut through part of it.

Frankie had wanted the refrigerator box they were using, but it was like Lila had known that Frankie wanted it and had run straight for it. Lila sure was fast. Now there were only boxes for smaller appliances, like ovens and washing machines.

It didn't matter, though. Frankie was the best inventor.

Ravi flattened down their dishwasher box. "If we keep it doubled like this, that should make it stronger, right?"

Frankie nodded. That, at least, was a good idea. "We should cross it, though," she said. "So the ripples are going different directions. That makes it even stronger."

She squatted down and cut the box into two even pieces. She cut off the flaps so they could use them for the front of the rocket. She was so intent on cutting straight lines that she didn't notice Lila, Suki, and Lauren come over until the other team was practically on top of them.

"A pencil sled?" Lila asked.

"That's kind of cool," Lauren said cheerfully.

"Yeah," Suki agreed. "You can dress all in yellow and match your sled. Maybe you could have some paper and—"

"It's not a pencil!" Frankie yelled.

The whole room quieted, and every single head swiveled to look at her. Frankie felt her cheeks go hot. Maya squirmed beside her.

Ms. Christine trotted over. "Everything okay over here?"

Everything was definitely *not* okay. Lila Jones and her team were cheating! Well, maybe not cheating, exactly, but they weren't playing fair. They were trying to get under Frankie's skin and—

Before Frankie could get her own thoughts straight, Lila said, "Frankie just started yelling at us."

"I wasn't yelling," Frankie said.

"You were yelling," Suki said softly. She wouldn't even look at Frankie, which made Frankie's cheeks burn more.

"Why were you even over here?" Frankie demanded of Lila. "Were you trying to copy us?"

Ms. Christine held up her hands. "Okay, let's cool our jets a minute. Remember what the goal is here?"

"To win the race," Frankie said. In her head she added: *And prove I really am the greatest third-grade inventor.*

Ms. Christine shook her head. "Three goals: teamwork, creativity, fun. Yelling is none of those—right, Frankie?"

Frankie was pretty sure that Lila was

smirking at her. She took deep breaths to calm down.

"So let's have everybody go back to their own spots and get to work," Ms. Christine added. "We have only ten more minutes until cleanup time."

Frankie watched Lila's back as she walked away. Frankie glowered. She glared. She sat in stony silence while Ravi and Maya taped the two parts of their base together.

If Lila Jones thought that she could throw Frankie Sparks off her game, she had another think coming.

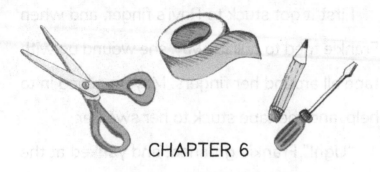

CHAPTER 6

The Trouble
with Tape

RRRRIIIIIIIIIP!

Frankie tore off a long strip of duct tape.
Ravi and Maya were holding two pieces of
cardboard together. Frankie's job was to pull
off long, thin strips of tape so they could stick
the two pieces of cardboard together for a
strong base.

The tape had other ideas.

First it got stuck to Ravi's finger, and when Frankie tried to pull it away, she wound up with tape all around her fingers. Maya reached in to help, and the tape stuck to her sweater.

"Ugh!" Frankie groaned, and yanked at the tape. She had worked with duct tape a lot. It was one of an inventor's greatest tools. But she usually worked with much smaller pieces. This was the third long strip they had ruined. She felt her face pinching up. Actually, she felt her whole body tensing, shriveling in on itself like a raisin.

They were back in the far corner of the room in the rec center for day two of building. All around the room, groups were working on their sleds. There were some second graders who were wrapping tape around the outside of a box over and over again. Luke, Ben, and Silas were still playing in their box, pretending to be Jedi fighting for the Rebel Alliance.

Then, of course, there were Lila, Suki, and Lauren. They were crowded around their sled, carefully adding strips of tape to the outside. They didn't seem to be having any trouble with the tape. Lila looked over her shoulder and caught Frankie watching her. Lila glared and then whispered something to Lauren.

"I think we might need another plan," Ravi said as he picked the last bits of tape off his finger.

"We have a good design," Frankie said, putting her hands on her hips. She was wearing her tool belt, and she peeked into the pockets to see if there was anything there to help them.

"It's just that these runners—they're really tricky," Ravi said.

"Tricky is how you get to impressive," Frankie told him. "Tricky leads to success."

"But we don't have a lot of time for this project," Maya said. "That's one of the things you need to consider when you're designing and inventing, right?"

Frankie scowled. Maya wasn't wrong. Before you started a design project, you had to consider things like what materials were available and how much time you had. But Frankie just couldn't give up on the runners. "The runners are our winning card," she said. "We have to keep them."

"Okay," Ravi said. "Then how about a different plan for putting tape on? What if we glued it first?"

"We can't use glue!" Frankie was exasperated. Had Ravi even looked at the rules? "This is the trouble with tape!" Frankie said. "It's just so sticky."

"They seem to have a good way of doing it," Maya said. She nodded toward Lila's group. It pained Frankie to admit it, but Maya

was right. And though it felt as awful as swallowing burrs, Frankie watched Suki and Lauren as they worked together. Suki unrolled the tape right onto the cardboard, and Lauren came behind her, pressing it down smoothly. Why hadn't Frankie thought of that? If she was such a great inventor, then she should know the best way to put on duct tape. But the other girls' tape was smooth and perfect, and hers was in a big wad at her feet.

Lila glared again. "Who's copying who now?" Lila asked. She had her honey-brown hair in a high ponytail that cascaded down her back. Frankie thought she looked like an evil queen from a fairy tale.

"You know," Ms. Christine said from the

front of the room, "I heard that at some of the big technology companies, they make sure that all the bathrooms are in a central location. You know why?"

Luke giggled and repeated the word "bathroom" like it was a joke all on its own.

Frankie, though, was curious.

Ms. Christine scooted off the table she'd been sitting on. "It's so that people who work in all different departments end up running into one another. They'll be walking across the building to get to the bathroom and see a friend, and it's like, 'Hey, Joe, what are you working on?' And 'Hey, Sally, I'm working on this really cool project.' And then Sally says, 'That is really cool, and it relates to what I'm doing.' So they talk and get ideas from one another." Ms. Christine paused for dramatic effect. "And you know what happens?"

Suki raised her hand, and Ms. Christine nodded at her. "They help each other out."

"Right!" Ms. Christine said. "And because they help each other, they both have better projects in the end."

Frankie scowled. She thought it was a smart design idea to force people to come together and talk. Frankie knew that all sorts of inventions happened when people got ideas from one another. And she also knew that Ms. Christine was trying to teach them a lesson.

As far as Frankie could see, though, Ms. Christine had it wrong. In her story, the people worked at the same company. That meant they were already on the same team. Frankie and Lila were not on the same team at all. Plus, Joe and Sally were working on totally different projects, but Frankie and Lila were both making sleds.

Frankie frowned down at their sled. "Let's try again," she said. Finally they got a piece down successfully. *One down,* Frankie thought, *about a million to go.*

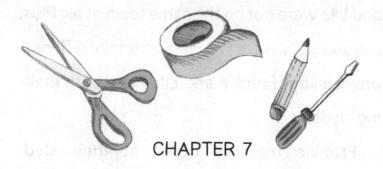

CHAPTER 7

The First Epic Failure

MAYA SAT IN FRONT, THEN FRANKIE, then Ravi. After a long afternoon of building the day before, only the base of their sled was finished, but Frankie thought they should test it. Ravi wore a pair of ski goggles. Frankie thought these were totally unnecessary. She knew it was best to test the sled in a low-stress situation first, so they were starting off on the baby hill at the park.

Unfortunately, Lila, Suki, and Lauren had had the same idea. Just as Frankie and her team had arrived, Lila's team had cruised by on their sled. Their sled looked like a square version of the bobsleds from the Olympics that Frankie had seen on the Internet. Frankie figured the girls had taken their refrigerator box and cut out a hole in the top for them to get through, then covered it all in brightly colored tape, like a rainbow. The sled wasn't very original, but it worked, and it went fast. As they'd whooshed by, their hair had shot back behind them.

Now Lila and the others were waiting at the bottom for Frankie, Maya, and Ravi to go. It felt to Frankie like the whole world was watching.

"Ready?" she asked. "One, two, three!"

The three friends used their hands to start their sled. Down, down, down . . . *splat*!

The sled dropped down and they stopped moving. They hadn't gone even three feet.

Frankie jumped out of their sled. Their runners had collapsed!

"Oh no!" she cried. "This is the worst thing that could've happened!"

Ravi and Maya looked at the sled, and then they looked at Frankie.

"It's fine, it's fine," Frankie said. "We just need to make them a little stronger."

"Or we could not use runners," Ravi said.

"We have to use runners!" Frankie exclaimed. How many times was she going to have to explain this to him? Real racing sleds had runners. Theirs would have them too.

"We don't *have* to," Ravi said. "You just really, really want to."

"We tried them, and we tested them, and they didn't work," Maya reminded Frankie. "So maybe now it's time to try something else."

"That's not how the test-and-retest phase of design works!" Frankie said. "You see what fails and then you fix the failures." She stomped her foot on the snow. At the bottom of the hill, Lila leaned over and said something to Suki. Frankie couldn't hear, but she was sure it wasn't nice. It was probably something like, *World's best third-grade inventor? Ha! More like world's worst inventor!*

Frankie's scowl felt big enough to take over her whole face. She couldn't stand there and watch as Lila laughed at her. She stormed off in the direction of the playground. Her feet made a satisfying *crunch, crunch, crunch* through the snow. She imagined she was walking on the moon, all by herself. It would be good to be 238,900 miles away from everyone else.

Those runners had been a good idea! No one else was going to try to build them, she was sure. That would make their sled stand out. Plus, they should have made the sled faster. Instead they'd made the sled fail. Normally Frankie didn't mind when her inventions didn't work the first time. That just meant she knew what she had to fix. "Failing forward," her mom called it. This felt like failing flat on her face.

She brushed the snow off a swing and sat down on it. She didn't feel like pumping, though. She just sat on the swing and looked at the snow and wished she would freeze into a snow sculpture. Kids would visit her and maybe put flowers at her frozen feet. They'd say, *Here sits Frankie Sparks. She was a great inventor once. Now she can't even make a sled.*

Frankie sniffed. The other good thing about

being a snow sculpture would be that her nose wouldn't run.

"Frankie?"

Frankie looked up. There was Maya, cheeks pink and eyes concerned. Behind Maya was Ravi, who still had the ski goggles on. He was holding their broken sled in one hand.

"Are you okay?" Maya asked.

Frankie shook her head.

Ravi flipped over the sled. "Only one of them broke. I think we can reinforce it and—"

Frankie shook her head. "It's useless!"

Maya looked over her shoulder at Ravi. He shrugged. Maya brushed off the swing next to Frankie and sat beside her. Ravi put the sled down and sat on it.

Maya rocked herself back and forth a little bit. "I thought failure was part of the process," Maya said.

"It *is*," Frankie said. "But this is an epic failure. This is a failure of monumental proportions. This is a failure you don't come back from."

"It was only one runner," Ravi reminded her. "Which means it was only a fifty percent failure."

Frankie groaned.

"What's going on, Frankie?" Maya asked. "You've been nothing but frustrated this whole time. Do you even want to do this contest?"

"Of course I do! It's just . . ." Frankie stopped. She wasn't sure what was bothering her. Ever since they'd made teams, Frankie had felt like a giant's thumb was pressing down on her chest, while a clock ticked louder and louder right inside her brain, where she couldn't turn it off. "I just don't like *this* invention. Sleds are a dumb thing to have a contest about anyway. There are a million different kinds. How are we supposed to come up with a new one? And one that is fast and has a good design? In only one week? It's absolutely ridiculous. Do you know how long it takes to make an invention? It took Lonnie Johnson years to perfect the Super Soaker. It took—"

"Stop!" Maya ordered.

Frankie snapped her mouth shut. Maya didn't normally yell, and Frankie was surprised.

"I think I know what's going on," Maya said. "This isn't about the sled failing. It's about the contest. It's about Lila."

"It is not—"

Maya shook her head. "Remember that big swim meet I had last year? When I had to go up against some of the fastest girls in the state?"

Frankie nodded. Maya had been terrified. Frankie had made her a special stuffed animal and programmed it to say "You can do it!" to make her feel better.

"You're acting the way I felt. You're thinking about the contest and about beating Lila.
You're not thinking about making a really cool
sled."

"But I *am*," Frankie protested.

"You know why our sled isn't working?"
Maya asked her.

"The runner broke," Frankie replied glumly.

"No." Maya shook her head again. "It's
because we aren't working together. I know
you really, really want to win, Frankie—"

"Really," Ravi stressed.

"But we aren't going to win if it's just your
ideas."

Frankie opened her mouth to protest, but
then she realized that maybe, just maybe,
Maya was right. Making a sled should have

been fun, and a chance to hang out more with her friends, but instead she was worried. She wanted to win. She especially wanted to beat Lila Jones. Sometimes competition was good for inventors, but other times it brought out the worst in people, like with Thomas Edison and Nikola Tesla. And right now, Frankie was acting like Edison, obsessed with making sure Tesla wouldn't beat him.

And Maya was right about something else: Frankie's ideas weren't enough. It was a team competition, and she had been acting like a team of one. This, at least, was a failure she knew how to fix. She jumped off the swing and turned to Ravi. "So," she said. "Who wants to go make a dragon?"

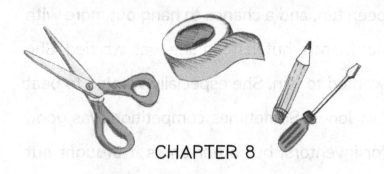

CHAPTER 8

Fixing Problems

"HERE!" FRANKIE EXCLAIMED, LOOKING at the bent runner. It was the next day and they were working in her basement, where they had placed the broken sled on the coffee table to examine what had gone wrong. Snow had gotten under the tape and weakened the cardboard.

"So the solution is more tape?" Maya asked.

"I think so."

Ravi looked up from his drawing of a

dragon head. "What color dragon do we want? Green or blue or red?"

Frankie had all sorts of ideas about what color the dragon should be, but she let Maya go first. "Purple," she said. "With a green belly."

Ravi picked up a colored pencil, and Frankie picked up a roll of green duct tape. "Let's get this belly started," she said.

They worked on the sled all afternoon. Fixing the bottom was easier now that they knew what had gone wrong. Frankie constructed a new runner, and Maya helped her attach it to the base. It turned out that Ravi and Maya were both great artists. The team drew and cut and taped until they had finished the dragon head for the front of the sled.

"I can't believe it!" Frankie exclaimed. "It

looks like a real dragon!" It had little yellow
horns, bright eyes, and sharp teeth. They had
put the tape on to look like scales.

"We should test our sled again," Maya said.

"Okay," Frankie said. "There's a little bit of a hill in my backyard. We can test it there."

Bundled into their snow gear, they placed their dragon sled at the top of the small hill and climbed in. It was hard for Frankie to see past the dragon's head, so she tilted her head to the side. "One, two, three, go!" she yelled.

They pushed off, and *whoosh*, down the slope they went. They jiggled and bounced over rougher patches of snow, and Frankie's belly felt like it had popcorn popping inside. They coasted to a stop right by her driveway.

"That was fast!" Maya yelled.

"But I bet we can be faster!" Ravi said.

"Let's do it!"

The three friends cheered and ran back up the hill.

They spent the rest of the week tinkering and testing, testing and tinkering. Ravi figured out how to lower the dragon's head so Frankie could see to steer. Frankie smoothed out the runners so there would be even less friction. They ran outside to try again.

"Whooaaaaa!" Ravi yelled as they came down the hill. The sled jiggled from side to side. Frankie felt like her insides were in a blender.

Thump, thump.

Ravi tumbled out the back. The sled coasted to a stop and Frankie jumped out. "Are you okay?" she asked.

Ravi popped up. "No major injuries to report!" he replied.

"We need to fix the wiggle in this sled," Frankie said.

"And make sure we don't fall out," Maya said. "Seat belts?"

Back to the basement! Frankie and Ravi added a center runner at the front to make the sled more stable. Maya taped two pieces of duct tape together to make a strap. Then she braided three straps together into rope. She used the rope to make handles for them to grab on to once the sled was moving.

"That's brilliant, Maya!" Frankie exclaimed. "Now none of us will fall out."

They hurried back outside to test the sled again.

In and out, in and out, all that afternoon, they tested and retested their sled. Frankie's mom and dad helped out by timing their runs. During each test run, the sled flew a little bit faster.

"That is one impressive dragon," Frankie's mom said. "But it's getting dark. Time to come inside."

That gave Frankie a great idea. "We could add lights!"

"Frankie!" Maya groaned, but with a smile.

"I think our sled's just about perfect," Ravi said. "We are ready for that race."

The team went inside, where Frankie's dad made them hot chocolate and cinnamon toast. "I think it's been scientifically proven that hot chocolate and cinnamon toast are the most perfect snack ever," Frankie declared.

"Really?" Ravi asked. "How could they possibly do that?"

Frankie laughed. "I was only kidding." Half her brain, though, was figuring out how to test her theory. That was just the way your brain worked when you were a great inventor.

Maya dunked her toast into her hot chocolate. "There's still one matter left to discuss," she said.

"What's that?" Frankie asked.

"Costumes!"

Frankie's and Ravi's faces lit up. Costumes weren't quite as much fun as inventing, but they were pretty close. The team put their heads together and whispered. It wasn't long before they had the perfect idea.

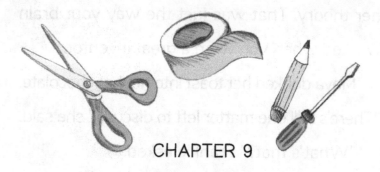

CHAPTER 9

The Race

FRANKIE, RAVI, AND MAYA STRAPPED their silver helmets onto their heads.

"Ready?" Frankie asked.

"Ready," Ravi and Maya agreed. They strode up the hill carrying their sled above them. They wore tunics over their snowsuits. They'd made their costumes out of felt and painted crests on them, just like old-fashioned knights. Maya's had a lion, Ravi's a dragon, and Frankie's an alien.

"And who do we have here?" Ms. Christine asked at the top of the hill.

"We are the Knights of Snowy Hill," Frankie replied seriously. "Right, guys?" she asked her team.

Maya and Ravi nodded. "Perfect!" Ravi said.

Ms. Christine smiled. "I thought your team was the Rocket Squad."

"We had a change of heart," Frankie said. She looked back at her teammates. "'Rocket Squad' was my idea, but this is *our* idea. Is it okay if we change it?"

"Of course!" Ms. Christine said. She crossed out the old name and wrote the new one on her clipboard, then told the kids to line their sled up with the others.

Lila, Suki, and Lauren were already there. They hadn't done much work on their sled. It was still the same boxy bobsled with rainbow decorations. Their costumes were pretty cool, though. Each wore two colors, one in front, one in back. When they sat down in their sled, they would look like a rainbow. Luke's team arrived in brown jumpsuits. Their sled was pretty much a flat letter *T*. Frankie had never seen so much tape on cardboard!

"It's an X-wing!" Luke explained happily to the crowd. "See, we all ride on our stomachs. I ride in the middle, and they each ride on a wing. Face-first! It's going to be epic."

It was like a three-person skeleton. It was awesome, and Frankie told them so. Now that her team had worked together on their idea, she could see the good in other people's ideas too.

The judges came around and made little notes as they examined each sled. Frankie chewed her lip nervously. She wished they could just get into their sleds and go!

Ravi petted the dragon's head. "You all set, little buddy?"

Finally it was time for the race to start. They climbed into their sled: Frankie, then Maya, then Ravi in the back.

"On your marks!" Ms. Christine announced. "Get set! Go!"

Frankie, Maya, and Ravi pushed off with their hands and then grabbed on to the handles that Maya had made. Their sled shot down the hill, as straight as an arrow. Faster, faster, faster they went, but the sled didn't jiggle and stayed on track.

"Hang on! Hang on!" Frankie heard Luke yelling from his sled. She peeked to the left. They were neck and neck! The boys' faces bounced just above the snow.

She peeked to the other side. She thought she saw a rainbow behind them, but everyone was moving too quickly!

"Woo-hoo!" Ravi yelled from the back of the sled.

"Charge!" Frankie yelled.

Maya and Ravi yelled it too. The three teammates tucked down more tightly in their sled.

Down, down, down they went. It was the

most exhilarating ride Frankie had ever been on. It was better than pumping the swings up to infinity on the playground, better than her saucer sled, better than the dragon flume ride or the corkscrew roller coaster at Adventure Fun Park! And they had made it themselves. That made it the very best of all.

Up ahead was the finish line. They were still neck and neck with Luke's team.

"Go, go, go!" Luke yelled.

"Charge!" Frankie yelled.

Luke's team edged a little bit ahead, then a little bit more.

The boys crossed the finish line first, with Frankie, Maya, and Ravi just behind.

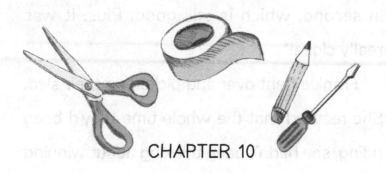

CHAPTER 10

Trophies

FRANKIE POPPED UP AND OUT OF
the sled.

"I'm sorry, Frankie," Maya said.

"What are you talking about?" Frankie
asked. She extended her hand and helped
Maya out of the sled. "That was the most stu-
pendously awesome sled ride ever."

"But we didn't win," Ravi said.

"That's okay," Frankie replied. "We came

in second, which is still good. Plus, it was really close!"

Frankie bent over and picked up their sled. She realized that the whole time they'd been riding, she hadn't been thinking about winning or Lila or any of that. She'd just had fun!

They walked over to the cocoa shed, where Ms. Christine was waiting next to three sets of trophies made out of cardboard and duct tape. Once all the racers were there, Ms. Christine cleared her throat. "Congratulations, racers! Our first annual cardboard-sled contest was a huge success!"

Everyone clapped and cheered.

"It is now time for me to announce our winners!"

Frankie's stomach flip-flopped, and her

heart beat a little faster. She guessed there was still a part of her that really wanted a trophy—and that was probably okay.

"First up, our fastest-sled trophy goes to Luke, Ben, and Silas."

Frankie clapped hard, her mittens making a satisfying *thunk, thunk, thunk* sound. The boys held their trophies above their heads while Ms. Christine took their picture.

"Nice race," Luke said to Frankie, Maya, and Ravi. "If we didn't have the Force on our side, you might have won."

"Live long and prosper," Ravi replied. That was from *Star Trek*, not *Star Wars*, but everyone laughed all the same.

"Next," Ms. Christine said, "we have the award for the best-looking sled."

Frankie crossed her fingers and toes. Sure, they hadn't won the race, but their design had been amazing. The front that really looked like a dragon, the handles, the runners—all of it.

"Our judges have conferred, and though it was close, we have a winner. . . ."

Luke pretended to beat out a drumroll on his legs.

Frankie leaned closer to Ms. Christine.

"The best-looking sled award goes to the Rainbow Girls!"

Lila, Lauren, and Suki began jumping up and down and squealing. It was, Frankie thought, very undignified. She herself fought to keep her emotions in check. *The Rainbow Girls? Really?* Had the judges not seen how carefully Ravi had made the teeth? How precise Maya's dragon scales were? Had they not considered the safety feature of handles or the stability of adding a center runner?

"It's okay," Maya whispered.

"Yeah, it's okay," Ravi said.

Ms. Christine ushered the Rainbow Girls back into the crowd. Frankie sniffled and stared at her snow boots.

"And now the most important award: our team-spirit award. This award goes to a team that faced some challenges, but pulled together and overcame those challenges as a team. They were hard to miss, in one of our most beautiful sleds today. They were runners-up in the speed challenge, were runners-up in design, and are first-place champions in team spirit: the Knights of Snowy Hill!"

Maya, Ravi, and Frankie grabbed on to one another and jumped up and down. Frankie might have even squealed, though in a very dignified manner. They ran up to Ms. Christine, who gave them each their trophy, then pulled them all in close for one big hug. "Great job, guys! I'm really proud of you!"

Frankie was really proud too. She had never won a team-spirit award before, and this one was perfect. Ms. Christine was almost as good with cardboard and tape as Frankie was herself.

After the trophies were given out, there was hot chocolate with marshmallows. Frankie drank hers and then wandered back up the hill. She looked out over the forest on the far side of town. In the summer she and her parents liked to come to this hill at night to observe the stars and planets. Frankie thought about that now, and about the rocket ship it would take to get to the stars.

As she stood there dreaming big dreams, Ravi and Maya came up the hill, carrying their dragon sled.

"Ahoy there, Sir Frankie!" called Maya.

"Are we pirates or knights?" Frankie asked.

"Pirate knights!" Ravi replied. *"En garde!"*

Frankie shook her head and laughed.

Maya asked, "Are you okay? We worried when you left the group."

"I'm great," Frankie said. "I was just thinking."

"About what?" Maya asked.

"I'm thinking about rockets," Frankie replied.

"And how our team could make a cardboard rocket that really flies!"

Maya laughed. "Oh, Frankie!"

Ravi smiled and said, "Why do we need a rocket when we have a dragon! Let's go!"

Ravi and Maya put the sled down at the top of the big hill.

"Are you sure about this, Maya?" Frankie asked. Maya had never wanted to go over Extreme Maximus before.

Maya nodded. "Before, I was scared, but with my fellow knights by my side, I will be courageous," she said solemnly.

The three friends got into the sled and gave themselves a big, huge, mammoth push down the hill. Their dragon gained speed. Faster, faster, faster. Frankie steered them right toward Extreme Maximus. Closer and closer they raced, and then . . . *wheeeee!* The Knights of Snowy Hill were airborne. Frankie was pretty sure that was the best feeling in the world.

The Design Process

Problem Identification

Brainstorm

Design

Test Retest

Share

Test, Test,
and Test Again

IN THIS STORY, FRANKIE, MAYA, AND
Ravi had to work together to build their sled.
Have you ever had to work in a group? It can
be really difficult! Frankie had to learn how to
listen to her friends and compromise.

Once Frankie, Maya, and Ravi had built
their sled, their work wasn't done. Designing and building are important parts of the

Test
Retest

process, but so are testing and retesting. Frankie and her friends kept racing their sled to see what was working well and what could be improved. They made sure no snow could get under the tape. They added a center runner for stability, and handles for safety. They ran tests to see if they could make their sled go faster. They kept working until they were happy with their sled, and then they brought it to the race.

This process of testing and retesting is essential in the design process.

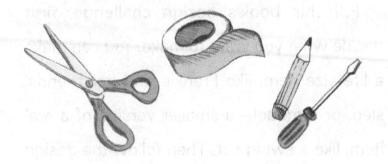

Your Turn to
Be the Inventor!

FRANKIE AND HER FRIENDS LOVE TO GO

sledding. What do you like to do? Do you play on

a swing set? How about playing video games?

Pretty much anything you can imagine, you can

build out of cardboard. Really! A nine-year-old

boy named Caine Monroy made a whole arcade

out of cardboard. You can visit his website and

learn all about it: www.cainesarcade.com.

For this book's design challenge, first decide what you want to make. You can make a life-size item, like Frankie and her friends' sled, or a model—a smaller version of a real item, like a swing set. Then follow the design process.

First, identify your problem. Sometimes in design the problem is simply identifying what you want to make. For example, at first Frankie wanted to make a sled that looked like a rocket. You can also think about making a thing better, like building a cooler swing.

Second, start brainstorming. What will it look like? What materials will you need? For this challenge, just like Frankie and her friends, you can use only cardboard and tape. If you don't have duct tape, any tape will do.

Masking tape is really easy to work with.

Next, design and build your item. Once you have it built, test it. Ask yourself: What worked well? What needs to be improved? Keep going through the build-test-retest cycle until you are happy with your product.

Finally, share your invention with friends and family.

Acknowledgments

Thank you to Margaret Burman for teaching me the best strategies for building with cardboard. Thank you also to my Dyer Dragon students, who always impress me with their creativity when building with cardboard and tape.

Thanks to my family, who give me time and space to create.

Just like Frankie, I'm lucky to have a good team at Aladdin who bring the books to life. Thank you to Alyson Heller, Elizabeth Mims, Karen Sherman, Laura Lyn DiSiena, Mike

Rosamilia, and Tiara Iandiorio. Thank you to illustrator Nadja Sarell, who captures Frankie and her friends so well.

Finally, a very special thanks to my agent, Sara Crowe.

Don't miss Frankie's next invention!

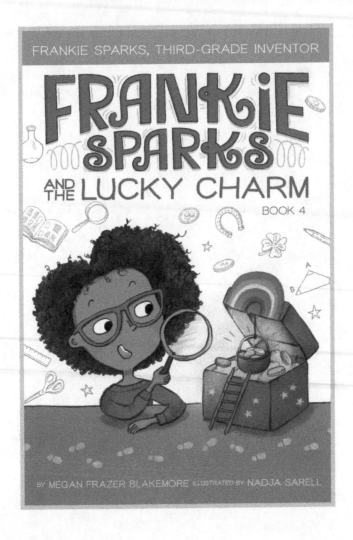

Don't miss Frankie's
next invention!

ARF! ARF!

When Frankie Sparks heard the dog, she smiled. She walked around Maya's house and into the backyard. Maya's dog, Opus, sprinted around the lawn. When he saw her, he barreled toward her, almost knocking her over.

"I'm teaching him to do tricks!" Maya explained. She stood in the center of the yard holding a Hula-Hoop.

"Is the trick 'knock down your best friend'?" Frankie asked with a laugh.

Frankie and Maya had been best friends

forever, and Frankie loved Maya's dog almost as much as she loved her own pet, a rat named Buttercup. Opus stopped and gave her a good sniff before starting to sprint again.

"He's supposed to jump through the hoop," Maya said with a shrug. "But mostly he runs around me and around the yard."

Frankie called Opus to her. He skidded to a stop at her side. "Maybe if you hold the hoop, and I call him from the other side, he'll jump through it." She told Opus to stay and then crossed Maya's lawn so Maya and the hoop was between her and Opus. It was early spring and the ground beneath her feet was squishy soft.

"Ready?" Frankie asked Maya.

Maya nodded.

"C'mere, Opus! C'mere boy!" Frankie called.

Opus's ears pricked up. *Arf!* He ran toward Frankie. Frankie clapped and called him again. She was certain Opus was going to jump right through the hoop.

Faster and faster Opus ran, right up to the hoop and then *swish*, Opus veered to the right, ran around the hoop, and then turned back toward Frankie. "No, Opus!" Frankie said. "Not like that."

"He's been doing that all afternoon. Just when I think he's going to do it—boom! He goes off in the other direction."

This sounded like a challenge, and there were few things that Frankie liked more than a challenge. "Hmm," she said. "Maybe if I were a little closer to the hoop."

They tried again with Frankie standing

closer to the hoop. Opus ran and ran and . . . skidded right under the hoop.

"No, Opus," Maya moaned.

Opus looked back at them with a confused expression on his face.

"It's okay," Frankie said. "You're a good dog." She turned to Maya. "He just doesn't know what we want him to do."

"Let's show him, then!" Maya said with a giggle.

Oh, no. Frankie knew where this was going.

"Come on, Frankie!" Maya called. "Go through the hoop!"

"Woof!" Frankie said. She jogged up to the hoop and stepped through.

"Good girl!" Maya said, and patted her on the head.

Arf! Opus said.

But when they called him through again, he just went around the girls. He sat down behind them. *Arf!*

"Opus!" the girls laughed.

Then Frankie snapped her fingers. "I've got it!" It really felt like a light bulb turning on when she got a good idea. Sometimes the light came all at once, like with a flick of a switch. Other times it was more like someone was turning up the light slowly, slowly, slowly. This idea came on all at once. "Hold the hoop on the ground," she said. "Then he can just walk right through. Then you can slowly raise it up until he's jumping through."

"Brilliant!" Maya said.

Brilliant was just about Frankie's favorite word.

Opus, though, had other ideas. When he got to the hoop, he barked at it, then he took off on his sprint around and around the yard.

"I guess some dogs just can't be taught tricks," Frankie said.

"It was a great idea, though," Maya told her.

They watched Opus go around and around. Then, all of a sudden, he dashed toward the garden shed in the back corner of the yard. He pressed his nose into the ground.

Arf arf! Arf arf arf arf arf!

"What is he barking at?" Frankie asked.

"Oh that's our leprechaun hole," Maya explained.

Frankie laughed. Maya must be joking, she thought. Everyone knew there was no such thing as a leprechaun.